Two Brown Bears

**Martin
Waddell**

**Illustrated by
Steve Lavis**

OXFORD
UNIVERSITY PRESS

OXFORD
UNIVERSITY PRESS

Great Clarendon Street, Oxford OX2 6DP

Oxford University Press is a department of the University of Oxford.
It furthers the University's objective of excellence in research, scholarship,
and education by publishing worldwide in

Oxford New York

Auckland Cape Town Dar es Salaam Hong Kong Karachi
Kuala Lumpur Madrid Melbourne Mexico City Nairobi
New Delhi Shanghai Taipei Toronto

With offices in

Argentina Austria Brazil Chile Czech Republic France Greece
Guatemala Hungary Italy Japan Poland Portugal Singapore
South Korea Switzerland Thailand Turkey Ukraine Vietnam

Oxford is a registered trade mark of Oxford University Press
in the UK and in certain other countries

British Library Cataloguing in Publication Data

Data available

ISBN-13: 978-0-19-919480-3
ISBN-10: 0-19-919480-7

9 10 8

Mixed Pack (1 of 6 different titles): ISBN 0 19 919483 1
Class Pack (6 copies of 6 titles): ISBN 0 19 919484 X

Printed in Hong Kong

Contents

Flying Bears

Chapter 1
The No-Wings Bear

One day, Harriet Bear was riding her bicycle.
She saw Joe Bear.

Joe was bouncing up and down,
up and down, flapping his arms.
"I'm trying to fly," explained Joe.
"Bears can't fly," Harriet said.

"Why can't bears fly?" asked Joe.

"They haven't got wings," said Harriet.

"But I *want* to fly in the sky," said Joe.
He sounded quite sad.

"I've got a Bear Plan," Harriet said. "I'll
make us a Bear Pedal Plane!"

Harriet made a list of the things that they would need.

Things that Bears need for
making Bear Pedal Planes
by Harriet Bear
Nails
Hammer
Wood
Saw
Some string
A big Sheet
One Bear bicycle
two extra bicycle chains
A Propeller
and one small Armchair
just big enough to fit Joe.

"LET'S DO IT!" said Joe.

Chapter 2

TAKE OFF!

They went to the top of Bear Hill.

First Harriet drew a picture of the
Bear Pedal Plane.

Then they made a frame for the plane, and two wings.

"Tie the frame on to my bear bicycle," Harriet said.

Joe tied the frame to the bicycle.

He ran the first chain down to the pedals.

Harriet fixed the second chain to the propeller.

"What's the armchair for?" Joe wanted to know.

"You sit there, and steer," Harriet said.

She fixed the bear armchair on to the frame.

The big sheet was tucked underneath, in case they might need it.

"My pedalling turns the propeller.
That's what makes the plane fly,"
explained Harriet Bear. "That's why this
is called a Bear Pedal Plane."

The bears put on their crash helmets.
They climbed into the Bear Pedal Plane.

"Now we free-wheel down the hill and fly off the big bump at the bottom," said Harriet.

"Right!" said Joe, getting excited.

"Hold on tight!" said Harriet, as they free-wheeled downhill.

"We're taking off, Joe!" yelled Harriet, as they came to the bump.

"Five, four, three, two, one, zero … BLAST OFF!" shouted Joe.

"We're in the air!" called Harriet, as they soared off the bump.

14

"Wheeee!" yelled Joe.

Harriet pedalled as fast as she could, to keep the plane up in the air.

They flew high in the sky, over the trees in Bear Wood.

"Look at me flying!" cheered Joe.

But …

"This is really hard work," grunted Harriet, pedalling hard.

Then …

"Oh dear," puffed Harriet.

"We've stopped flying!" cried Joe, looking down at the ground.

"I'm a bust bear!" gasped Harriet. "I'm so puffed I can't pedal!"

"We're going to crash land on the trees in Bear Wood," yelled Joe.

The plane headed straight for the ground.

Chapter 3

Harriet Has a Plan!

"Save me, Harriet!" wailed Joe.

"I'm thinking as fast as I can," said Harriet.

"Then think faster," said Joe.

"I've got it!" said Harriet. "Use the big sheet I put under your chair. It will be our bear parachute."

"I *knew* you'd have a Plan!" gasped Joe.
And that's what they did.

It was the best two-bear parachute ever,
invented by Harriet.

The bears landed in Mother Bear's
cabbage patch.

"What have you been doing?" asked Mother Bear.

"Joe wanted to fly, so we flew," said Harriet.

"Don't be silly," said Mother Bear. "Bears can't fly."

"WE JUST DID!" said Joe.

Joe Bear Goes Exploring

Chapter 1

Joe Bear Reads a Book

One day, Joe Bear got a book from the Library Bus. The book was about bear explorers.

Joe Bear read it all in one go before he had his tea.

He read it again after his tea.

Then he went looking for Harriet Bear.

"We're having a Bear Expedition," he told Harriet Bear. "We're going where no bear has been before.

"I will be leader. I have to go first because I thought of it. I've read all about it in my library book."

They went to a part of Bear Wood where they'd not been before.

The trees there were tall and dark.
They blotted out most of the moonlight.
   "Are you there, Harriet Bear?" asked
Joe Bear, turning around.

"I'm right behind you,"
said Harriet Bear.

The further they went into Bear Wood
the darker it was. Brambles spread all
over the path.

They had to push their way through.

"Just follow me," said Joe Bear. "I am
your leader."

"Is that so?" said Harriet Bear.

"Yes, it is," said Joe Bear, proudly.

Harriet Bear looked around her.
She'd never been that way before.
"Which way do we go?" she asked.

"Don't bother me now," said Joe Bear.
He sounded very important. "I have to be
sure that we're on the right path."

They walked a bit more.

"Where are we now?" asked Harriet
Bear. "We have to be home before
bedtime, Joe Bear."

"Ha-ho-ha-hum," said Joe Bear, pretending that he hadn't heard her.

They came to a place where two paths crossed.

Joe Bear stopped and looked around. He didn't know which way to go.

"Are we lost, Joe Bear?" said Harriet Bear.

And they were.

Chapter *2*

Joe Bear Climbs a Tree

"We might need one of your Bear Plans to get us safe home, Harriet Bear," said Joe Bear.

They both stood very still.

Harriet worked on her Plan.

"Can you find a big tree for me?" asked Harriet Bear.

"There's one over there,"
said Joe Bear.

"Well spotted, Joe Bear,"
said Harriet Bear.

"What do I do with the
tree?" asked Joe Bear.

"Can you climb it?" asked
Harriet Bear.

"I'm a brown bear," said
Joe Bear. "I'm the best climber
there is."

He climbed to the top of
the tree, and looked down
below.

"Can you see the moon
from up there?" called
Harriet Bear.

"The moon's over there,"
said Joe Bear. He pointed.

"Your house is at the end
of the wood where the moon
rises," said Harriet Bear.
"The moon-path will take us
straight home."

29

Joe Bear climbed down from the tree.

"This way!" he shouted. "Just follow me, Harriet Bear."

Harriet Bear followed Joe Bear through the trees.

"Hurry up, Harriet Bear," said Joe Bear. "We have to get home before bedtime."

"Almost home now!" called Joe Bear.

When they got to Bear Cottage,
Mother Bear was waiting.

"Where have you been?" asked Mother
Bear.

"We've been where no bear has been
before," said Harriet Bear.

"I looked after Harriet Bear," said Joe
Bear.

"That's just what you did," said Harriet
Bear. "You brought us safely back home."

About the author

The "Exploring" story came first.

I'd listened to a slightly older child letting a smaller child seem to win a word game, and I'd watched the moon hang over the trees in the woods near my house.

Suppose two little bears were out in the woods, and the smaller bear believed he was lost ... how could the bigger bear help him solve his problem?

Looking and listening ... that's how I find stories.